Elkie Kammer

The White Elk

A Story from the Far North

© Elkie Kammer

First published in 2013 by
For The Right Reasons
(Charity no. SC037781)
Printers & Publishers
60 Grant Street, Inverness

British Library Cataloguing in Publication Data.
A catalogue record of this book is available
from the British Library.

ISBN: 978-1-905787-77-7

Cover design and illustrations by Elkie Kammer

Chapters:

1) The Fight

Andy flung his school bag over his shoulder and ran to catch up with the other children on the dusty road. He was always last even though he only had a short way to come. Just before he reached the school gate, he met up with a small group of boys.

"Impossible!" was the first word he caught. "Only rabbits and mice can get out; not a fully-grown elk!" As soon as he heard the word "elk", Andy knew what they were talking about.

"It's true!" he shouted. "My uncle saw him with his own eyes up on the Borgefell. His coat's as white as snow and his antlers are huge!" Andy stretched out his arms as far as they would reach. "It must be the one from the National Park. There's no other elk like that in the whole of Norway."

"Your uncle must have been seeing things. He was probably drunk as usual," Chris laughed. "Nothing as big as an elk can escape from the Park, unless he thought he was a cloud and managed to fly." He spread out his arms like wings, pretending to take off.

Andy was trembling with anger. His eyes burning with fire, he turned to Chris and snapped: "Don't you dare make fun of my uncle! He can see a lot better than your goggle-eyes daddy!"

"Well, maybe he needs an eye test and get a pair of glasses so he knows what's in front of him," Chris sneered.

Meanwhile the group had reached the big gate that led into the playground. Andy was furious now. "My uncle knows what he has seen!" he spat. "Why don't you go and look for yourself?"

Chris took a deep breath and sighed. "Only an idiot would run up a mountain, looking for the mirage of a drunk."

That was too much for Andy. He dropped his bag and pulled up his sleeves. Without another word he shot his fist into Chris's face, but Chris ducked and was only slightly caught on his cheek. He, too, got rid of his school bag and made ready to fight.

"Pea-brain!"

"Numb-skull!"

The swear words flew forward and backward while the boys were dancing around each other, their fists ready to attack. Suddenly Andy hit out again, catching Chris's ear. Chris took revenge and threw his fist into Andy's jaw. The fight became serious as both of them were now possessed by anger and driven by the shouts of the onlookers who enjoyed the show.

Nobody was surprised to see Andy involved in a fight. What else did he learn from his dad who was known for his quick temper! Chris, however, was different. As the minister's son and being clever with words, he didn't usually need his fists to hammer his point in. Today it was different, though. Soon the boys were on the ground in a cloud of dust, which made it difficult for the other children to see what was happening. The swear words had long stopped and all that could be heard was an occasional "Huh!" and "Argh!" and "Ouch!"

Although Chris was almost a head taller and heavier built, Andy managed to get on top of him. Just when he was sure of his victory, Chris threw him off again and scrambled to his feet. At that moment Andy clawed at Chris's ankle. Chris tried to steady himself, but he lost his balance. Like a tree under the axe of a wood cutter, he toppled to one side, his face scraping the gate post while he fell. His scream was drowned by the noise of the onlookers. Once more Andy knelt on top of his enemy, but he noticed that Chris was no longer fighting.

"Do you give up, rat-face?" he hissed in his ear. Instead of an answer Andy noticed a dark stream seeping out from under Chris's head. He was startled. Had Chris got seriously hurt? But no, it was probably just a nose bleed or a split lip. The fact that he lay so still with his hands pressed against his face only showed his shame. Chris wasn't used to being defeated. Or perhaps it was a trick and as soon as Andy moved, he would hurl himself onto him again.

But Andy wasn't tricked that easily. "Say that you give up and I'll leave you alone," he demanded. Suddenly, one of the onlookers who had bent forward to see where the blood was coming from, cried: "His eye! Look at his eye!"

Andy decided to get up and turn his enemy over. When he saw Chris's face, he felt the blood drain from his head and thought he was going to faint. The left eye had been torn from its socket and turned the side of Chris's face into an ugly mess. Andy looked up at the gate post which was responsible for the wound. He was still staring at it when some children returned with a teacher. Andy no longer noticed what was going on around him. The voices and screams seemed to come from far away and have nothing to do with him. Finally, even the gate post vanished from his sight. All he could think about was: "It's my fault. If Chris loses his eye, it's my fault." And suddenly he turned and ran away.

2) Whose Fault?

First his legs carried him straight home but, when Andy arrived at the garden gate, he didn't dare to go through. What would his mum say when he came back from school before it had even started? Of course she would question him about what had happened and, as soon as she knew, he'd be doomed. Andy felt his knees turn into jelly. He mustn't stand around. He had to run away from the village and the people who were sure to get him for what he had done. Just when he turned from the gate, his mum's face appeared at the kitchen window. Andy didn't see her and neither did he hear her calling after him. He made straight for the woods and ran on and on until he was out of breath.

Exhausted, he sank onto a patch of moss. His whole body was shaking, as the image of Chris's bloody face didn't leave him alone. He felt like screaming, but his throat was so dry that it only let out a hoarse growl. Suddenly, he heard a noise in the forest behind him. Andy jumped and turned round, but he couldn't see any movement. Were they searching for him? Did he

have to go to prison if Chris's eye couldn't be fixed?
The way his eyeball had dangled above his cheek,
Andy didn't think he would ever be able to see again.

"I didn't mean it!" he screamed in his head for the umpteenths time. "How could I know he'd fall against the gate post? He started it by calling Uncle Eddy a drunken liar! It was his own fault!" But as much as he tried to defend himself, he couldn't shake off the feeling of guilt. After all, it had been Andy who landed the fist blow and it had been his hands that caused Chris to lose his balance and hit the post. Andy once more collapsed onto the patch of moss. He buried his face and hands in the damp green stuff and finally let his tears flow freely.

Andy couldn't tell how long he had been crying. It felt like hours, but might have been only minutes, when he suddenly heard someone call his name. He lifted his head and held his breath. There it was again, his mum's voice ringing through the woods. "Does she know what happened?" Andy wondered. He spied through the branches to see if he could make her out. "Andy, where are you?" Her voice was coming closer. What was she going to do with him? Hand him over to the police? Would they lock him up in one of those Juvenile Detention Centres for dangerous kids?

Whatever, Andy was sure there was nothing but trouble waiting for him in the village. He crawled into the undergrowth and quietly slipped away from the voice that was calling his name.

After a while the trees thinned. Andy heard water splashing down some rocks and the next moment he stepped out onto the open fell. He had been out on the hills before, but never alone. He knew they went on and on, getting steeper and rockier and, when the clouds moved in, one could easily get lost up there. But today the sky was blue. A light breeze ruffled Andy's hair and the water in the burn sparkled in the sun. Andy was tired. He would have liked to rest for a while and think about a plan. How long could he survive up here without food and warm clothes? It was still too early in the year for berries and mushrooms and he didn't have a weapon to go hunting. The thought of killing an animal suddenly brought back the horrible image of Chris's bloody face. A shudder went down his spine and without command his legs carried him onwards into the wilderness.

Eventually, Andy had to sit down and rest. He was hungry as well as tired. It must be past lunch time and he was miles away from anyone. Andy leaned against a rock, his eyes scanning the barren hillside and resting on the dark wood far below him. Somewhere behind those trees was the village. Andy didn't want to think of the people and what had happened that morning. So he turned round to face the hills above him. The sun warmed his face and made him sleepy.

The next thing Andy was aware of was the bars on a window. Looking around, he found himself in a narrow prison cell with a bucket in one corner and a dirty mattress in the other. He felt panic rise in his chest when he noticed the heavy bolted door. "I have to get out here!" was his first thought. He tried to jump up, but something was holding his legs down. "Let me out!" he tried to scream, but his mouth wouldn't open.

Suddenly he saw a face at the window, an ugly one-eyed monster staring down at him. It took Andy a minute to realise that it was Chris's face. He wanted to close his eyes, but something was forcing his eyelids open. "Leave me alone!" he wanted to shout.

"Go away! It wasn't my fault! You started it!" At that moment Andy's head connected with something hard and he jerked awake from his nightmare. He was still sitting by the rock up on the fell. They hadn't locked him up yet. Andy took a deep breath and let out a sigh.

"It wasn't my fault," he whispered. "We were both fighting and it was an accident." Clearly, people must know that he hadn't ripped Chris's eye out on purpose! They had no right to lock him up. It could easily have been him losing an eye or an ear in the fight. Would Chris have had to go to prison for that?

Suddenly Andy felt different. "What am I doing up here? Why did I run away?" He straightened his back, allowing a trace of defiance to push through his feelings of guilt. "Surely, it isn't my fault. It could have happened to anyone." Although his conscience wasn't easily won over, Andy managed to persuade himself that he had nothing to fear. They couldn't lock him up for an accident. People might be angry with him and blame him, but that was nothing new. Andy had never been popular, so what?

While he began to retrace his steps he constantly reminded himself that he was innocent, that the whole thing had been an accident and that he was not to blame. By the time he reached the village his steps had become almost firm. The only thing that bothered him was explaining to his mum why he had run away. If he knew he was innocent, he surely didn't have a reason to take off like that.

"I can tell her that I felt sick and needed the fresh air," he finally decided.

Andy noisily opened the garden gate and stomped up the steps to the front door. Nobody needed to think that he was creeping around with a guilty conscience. He kicked his shoes off when the kitchen door opened and his sister came out. She stared at him as if he was a ghost.

"What's wrong?" Andy snapped. "I needed fresh air, so I went for a walk." He pushed past her into the kitchen. "Where's mum?" he asked.

"She's been out looking for you all day," Helga said quietly. Andy leaned against the kitchen table. "Stop staring at me!" he suddenly shouted. "Do I look like a monster or something?"

Helga turned her face to the window. "They rushed Chris to hospital," she said, trying hard to keep her voice calm. "He's having an operation to rescue his eye."

"What's that got to do with me?" Andy burst out. "He shouldn't have called Uncle Eddy a drunk, and anyway, it was an accident." His words sounded hollow, even to himself, and there was the image of Chris's face again with the eye hanging loose and blood running down his cheek. Andy had to sit down as his legs threatened to buckle under him.

"I wish you'd at least feel sorry," Helga said quietly, still looking out the window.

"What do you mean?" Andy shouted. Then he added somewhat calmer: "Of course, I feel sorry for him, but it's not my fault. He could've fallen any time against that stupid gate post and lost his eye."

Helga slowly turned round. "But it happened when you pulled at his legs and made him lose his balance."

Andy jumped from his chair. "Shut up!" he screamed. "You only want to get me into trouble, but I say it once and for all: It wasn't my fault!" He stormed out of the kitchen and made for the stairs, almost falling over his school bag. "Helga must have taken it home for me," he thought, while he picked it up and went to his room.

3) Shunned

For the last three years Andy's dad had been working in town. Their small farm couldn't really support them, so he had to take a job in a tractor factory. This meant that he only came home for the weekend. Quite a few families had left the village when farming brought in less and less income. Most of them had moved away altogether, but Andy's mum refused to leave the house in which she had grown up.

"Anyway, we can still grow enough food for ourselves, and it's much better out here for the children than living in town," she had added.

When he was younger, Andy had helped his dad on the farm and they had done other things together, like fishing and exploring the woods or building things. But now dad was always tired and grumpy when he came home for the weekend and Andy usually tried to avoid him.

The day Chris lost his eye was a Wednesday. Andy was still in his room when he heard the front door open.

"Is Andy back?" he heard his mum calling in the hallway.

The kitchen door opened and Helga replied: "Yes, he's up in his room. Any news about Chris?"

"His mother told me the eye is lost, but they're hoping it doesn't leave any brain damage." She sighed. "Oh, my God! Why did it have to come to that?" Andy could hear her crying and Helga would probably join in any minute.

"Lost. His eye's lost…" Andy thought. "He's still got his other eye, though." He squeezed his left eye shut to find out what the world looked like with only his right one. He could still see, but only half as much. Once again his guilty conscience crept up on him. "Chris will never be able to see properly again and it's your fault." He swallowed. If only he could turn the time back to before the fight and make things undone! But, of course, he couldn't do that. Instead, he tried to ease the burden of guilt by going back into defence mode.

"It could have happened any time to anyone. Why did they have to put such a stupid gate post there?" He picked up his school bag and began to sort it out for the next day.

"It's not my fault. It was an accident. They can't blame me for an accident," he reasoned in his mind. "Anyway, he shouldn't have made fun of Uncle Eddy. I'm sure the white elk is really out there."

Andy was just closing his school bag when he heard steps on the stairs. A moment later the door opened and his mum came in. She looked at him as if she had never seen him before.

"What do you want?" Andy asked, but he couldn't meet her eyes. It seemed ages before his mum finally opened her mouth. "I was looking for you all day," she said quietly. "Where have you been?"

Andy swallowed. "I felt sick and needed some fresh air. That's why I went for a walk," he said without conviction.

His mum nodded. "Yes, you must have felt sick after what you did to Chris," she agreed.

"What do you mean?" Andy flared up. "We had a fight and he accidentally knocked against that gate post! It's not as if I gauged out his eye with my own hands!" He kicked his school bag under his bed and went over to the window.
"Look at me," his mum said, but Andy didn't turn round. So she stepped forward and took hold of his shoulders.

"Andy, look at me!" she said again, louder, but Andy shook her hands off and banged his fist on the windowsill.

"It's not my fault! He shouldn't have called Uncle Eddy a drunk! Serves him right for always making fun of us!" he shouted.

"Andy, how can you say this?" his mum sounded shocked. "What has become of you, Anders Larsen?" She shook her head as if to say: "Are you really my son?" Andy folded his arms over his chest and stared defiantly out of the window.

"Wait until your father comes home. Perhaps he'll be able to beat some sense into you." With that, his mother turned and left his room. When she was out of earshot, Andy collapsed onto his bed and for the second time that day he allowed his tears to flow freely.

Next morning Andy took ages to get ready for school. In the end he had to run and arrived just after the bell had gone. When he sat down in his seat, Henning, who shared the desk with him, moved away to the edge. Andy looked at him for a moment before he lifted his eyes to the empty seat everybody was staring at. Chris's seat. Of course, he was still in hospital. Mr Paterson, their teacher, took the register. The class was unusually quiet.

Once the lunches were sorted, Mr Paterson looked them over and said in a solemn voice: "I know, it's hard to believe what happened yesterday." He slowly shook his head. "Our thoughts are with Christian, whose life will never be the same again."
Andy swallowed. Although he was staring at his desk, he could feel the silent accusations of his classmates burning into him.

"Let's hope that the doctors will be able to restore his face as best as possible," Mr Paterson carried on. "And let's all learn from this incident, especially you, Anders, that there are better ways to solve arguments than using your fists."

Suddenly a girl behind Andy piped up: "It wasn't just an incident, Mr Paterson. Andy made him deliberately smash into the gate post. He did it on purpose."

Andy jumped up and turned to the girl. "Rubbish! It was an accident! I didn't put that daft gate post there!"

"But you grabbed Chris's legs, so his face would smash into it," someone else put in. More children gave their opinion, and it was soon clear to Andy that they all blamed him for what had happened to Chris. Andy had never been popular, but now he felt outright rejected. They hated him. They wanted him thrown out and put in jail.

In the end Mr Paterson called for silence, but later in the playground the taunting carried on. First Andy tried to ignore their comments. He kept to himself, kicking a small stone around. Two girls passed him, hissing: "Beast!" and "Psycho!" at him. In his anger, Andy kicked the stone harder than he had meant. It shot through the air and nearly hit a little boy.

"Hey!" someone shouted. "Is one eye not enough? Are you trying to make us all blind?"

Andy was trembling with rage. He knew he should ignore the nasty comment, but he had swallowed too much already. So he picked up another stone and threw it in the boy's direction. The next moment, someone grabbed him from behind and twisted his arms onto his back.

When Mr Paterson came out to take his class in, he had to break up another fight.
"Don't you think you've done enough harm?" he spat at Andy after separating him from his opponent. "How many more children do you want to maim?"
Andy threw his head back and scowled defiantly. The last thing he needed was to break down and cry.
"I see, you don't care about others," Mr Paterson misinterpreted Andy's hard mask. Then he shook his head and hissed: "Get out of my sight!"
Andy gladly did just that. Instead of following the others into the building, he turned and ran off.

4) Punishment

Friday evening, Andy nervously paced up and down in his room, listening to the sounds from the kitchen. As usual, his mum was cooking a special dinner to welcome dad home for the weekend. The delicious smells were already wafting up the stairs. But Andy had mixed feelings about the festive meal. As soon as his dad heard about the trouble Andy was in, even the best food in the world wouldn't calm his anger. Andy had already played with the idea of hiding in the woods to avoid his dad, but the nights were still too cold for sleeping out and he couldn't hide forever. Eventually, he'd have to face his dad; so better get it over with now.

The barking of the neighbour's dog announced the arrival of the bus. Andy held his breath when he heard the squeaking of the garden gate. Helga ran to open the door. She had always been fond of dad and managed to please him, even when he was tired and grumpy. Andy listened to the greetings downstairs. How long before they mentioned the fight with Chris and his running away from school?

Suddenly, Andy heard footsteps on the stairs. It was definitely the heavy gait of his dad. Andy felt his knees turn to jelly and, before they could give way under him, he sat down on the edge of his bed.

His dad didn't bother to knock at the door. He simply opened it and came in. Standing with his legs apart and his arms crossed over his chest, he looked down at Andy and roared: "What did I hear about you, son?" Andy knew that he wasn't waiting for an answer, so he kept quiet.
"Turning into a bully, are you? Knocking people's eyes out and then calling it an accident, huh?" He suddenly lunged forward and pulled Andy to his feet. "What do you think you are doing?" he shouted in his face.
"Have you lost your marbles or something? Want to end up in prison?" He shook Andy so hard that his neck hurt, but still Andy didn't make a sound.
"Bastard!" his dad finally spat and threw him onto the bed. "To think that my own son behaves in such a shameful way!" He shook his head. "I'll teach you! I'll make sure this doesn't carry on! For now you can stay in your room while we enjoy our dinner. A disgrace you

are! An utter disgrace!" He turned and left the room, slamming the door shut behind him.

The weekend carried on as it had begun. Although Andy did his best to avoid his dad, his contempt followed him everywhere. He did his chores on the farm, knowing that nothing was good enough to earn him praise. Even his mum and Helga treated him like an outcast. Had it not been so wet, Andy would have fled into the woods just to get out of their way. He felt utterly miserable, and part of him even thought that he deserved it.

Before his dad left on Sunday night he took Andy aside again.

"Listen," he began, "don't you dare bring anymore shame on our family! No more truancy and no more fighting, you hear me? Or else I'll have to resort to harder measures to get you back on the right track. Do you get it?" Andy nodded, but his dad wanted a proper answer. "Do you get it?" he asked again.

"Yes, dad," Andy said quietly, fighting back the tears.

5) Trying to make amends

The following week Andy did his best to stay out of trouble. He ignored the nasty comments of his classmates and burrowed himself in his school work instead. During break times he hid somewhere behind the buildings and, when his anger threatened to explode, he dug his nails into his skin or bit his lip until it was bleeding.

At home, mum and Helga started to be kinder to him again, but he could still feel their doubts hanging in the air. "What's got into him, fighting like that? Is this Andy, our son and little brother?" They weren't exactly scared of him, just wary, as if they didn't trust him anymore.

Andy managed to keep his head down for another couple of weeks. The weather was getting warmer and the days longer, but without friends he didn't really enjoy being out and about. He wasn't even sure if he was looking forward to the long summer holidays. It would be a very lonely time.

Then, almost a month after the fight, Chris came back. When Andy saw his face, he felt sick. The surgeon had obviously done a good job filling the empty socket with an artificial eye, and the skin around it was healing well. But the lifeless stare couldn't disguise the fact that the real eye was gone.

Chris still had to get used to the fact that he was half-blind. He frequently bumped into things and always got a fright when someone approached him from the left side. He was also slightly dazed from the painkillers and other medication and only managed to attend morning lessons at first.

Andy swallowed and concentrated on his breathing to stay calm. Would he get used to Chris's face or would it be a daily reminder of that fateful fight?

Chris stayed away from Andy. He never openly blamed him for what had happened as the other children had done. He simply ignored him and in a way that was worse. Andy would have liked to talk to him, to tell him how sorry he felt, to offer his help or anything else to make amends, but the others made sure he had no chance to approach him.

That evening, Andy stood in his room, looking at all his precious possessions. There was his fishing rod with a box of shiny flies Uncle Eddy had given him for his last birthday. But Chris wasn't really into fishing. What about his Lego models or his little racing cars or his precious stone collection? Andy sighed. No, Chris had much better stuff at home. He'd probably laugh at him for offering him his old toys. Suddenly, he remembered his set of woodcarving tools. He crawled under his bed where he kept the box, together with some half-finished carvings, and opened the lid. His eyes immediately rested on his pocketknife, a Christmas present from his dad which he treasured more than anything else. It meant a lot to Andy, not only because of its sharp stainless steel blade and the horn encasing. It was the best present ever, and his dad had bought it especially for him. Surely Andy couldn't just give it away? Perhaps he could save his pocket money until he had enough to buy one for Chris. But no, that would take far too long. He needed something now. He had to let Chris know how bad he felt about his eye, and what better way than to give him his most precious possession?

All night Andy battled with the thought of parting with his special knife. The arguments went to and fro in his head like a ping-pong ball on a table. In the end he fell into an exhausted sleep but, even in his dreams the pocketknife appeared, causing him grief. By morning he still hadn't come to a decision. Finally he slipped the knife in his pocket and hurried to school.

As usual, Henning made sure to leave a gap between him and Andy, though he would rather have moved to another table altogether. Most children treated him like thin air, while a few whispered nasty comments to him, but by now Andy had learned to ignore them. He got out his language jotter and his pencil case, ready for the lesson ahead. However, his thoughts started to wander away as soon as Mr Paterson explained about irregular verbs. Andy glanced across to Chris while his left hand cradled the knife in his pocket. "I have to catch him on his own," Andy reasoned, "or else his cronies won't let me near him." Should he follow

Chris home at lunch time? But that might be seen as playing truant again.

Half-way through the lesson Chris suddenly put his hand up and asked to go to the toilet. Mr Paterson let him go. While Chris carefully made his way to the door, Andy saw his opportunity.

"Please, may I go to the toilet?" he piped up. "I'm bursting." He was already on his feet, when Mr Paterson shouted: "No, you can wait! In fact, first you can show me what's in your pocket that you've been fiddling with all morning."

Andy's heart missed a beat. Show Mr Paterson what was in his pocket? The teacher came down the aisle and stopped in front of him. He held out his hand. Andy hesitated. Now he would be in real trouble. Not only were knives banned from school, but what would Mr Paterson think Andy was going to do with it? He slowly brought his hand out of his pocket, clutching a piece of dirty tissue. "I... I've only got..." he stammered.

"Now show me what else is in your pocket," Mr Paterson interrupted him. Andy had no choice. It was obvious that his pocket contained more than the dirty tissue. His trembling fingers unearthed the pocketknife and let it glide into Mr Paterson's outstretched hand.

A sigh went through the class, which was followed by shocked silence. "I can't believe this," Mr Paterson whispered. Andy wanted to explain that it was his most precious possession and that he had intended to offer it to Chris as a present to show that he was sorry, but the words were stuck in his throat.

"I'll better keep this until your father comes home," Mr Paterson said, weighing the knife in his hand. "And

I thought you had taken things to heart..." He slowly walked back to his desk. Chris opened the door and, without waiting for permission, Andy ran all the way to the toilets and just made it before he was sick.

The rest of the week Andy spent in a state of dread. What were they all thinking of him? That he was a psychopath going round torturing people? Why would nobody believe him?

Well, he did manage to explain the whole thing to his sister, and Helga knew him well enough to understand that he was telling the truth. She had promised to talk to mum and even to Mr Paterson, but Andy doubted that the teacher would change his mind about him. To him, as to the rest of the class, Andy was a criminal who should be locked up in a safe place before he could do more harm.

This time his dad decided that Andy needed stronger methods to reign in his behaviour. First of all, he kept the pocketknife and confiscated Andy's box of woodcarving tools. Then he made him write a letter of apology to Mr Paterson for bringing the knife to school. And finally he marched him all the way to the manse to formally ask forgiveness for what he had done to Chris. "Never mind if it was an accident," he insisted. "Had it not been for you grabbing his legs, Chris wouldn't have lost his eye."

Andy nearly forgot what to say when he stood in front of the minister and his wife. Chris refused to come out of his bedroom, so he could only recite his apology to his parents. They listened, nodding quietly, his mother dabbing at tears, his father too grieved to absolve him.

For the rest of the weekend Andy had to do all sorts of extra chores, which he didn't mind too much since he had no friends to play with.

6) Buying Friends

There was a rather plump girl in Andy's class, called Ingrid. He had never really noticed her before, but now that Andy was shunned by his classmates, he realised how lonely Ingrid must feel. The other girls either made fun of her or shut her out. In PE nobody wanted her on their team because she was so slow and clumsy, and in other group work she was sidelined and her contributions were never taken seriously.

Although Andy was good at sports, since the fight with Chris he always got chosen last and his team-mates didn't really include him in the game.

In Ingrid's case there was one exception regarding her popularity, and that was when she had sweets to share.

Ten days before the summer holidays Ingrid brought a huge bag of candy bars to school. It was her eleventh birthday and she went through the class, offering everybody a treat.

Later in the playground everybody wanted to be her friend. The girls shared their skipping rope with her and even admired her new hair band, while the boys cast her friendly smiles and commented on her generosity. Of course, they were only after her candy bars, but this gave Andy an idea.

When he came home, he went straight up to his room and opened his piggy-bank. Altogether he counted seven kroner seventy five. "That's just enough for two big chocolates," he thought, disappointed. But then he shrugged his shoulders. "Better than nothing." He put the money in his pocket and went out again.

There was only one shop in the village which sold everything from fishing gear to stationary, food and some clothes. When Andy entered, the shopkeeper, Mrs Sorvik, was in deep conversation with another old lady and didn't pay him much attention. Andy went straight to the sweets aisle. He looked at the prices and shook his head. "What a rip off!" he thought. "For three kroner I should get at least two of those big chocolates." He glanced around him to make sure nobody was watching and quickly tucked one of the chocolates under his jumper. Then he took another one over to the check-out. The two women were still busy talking, so Mrs Sorvik just took his money and let him go.

Back in his room, Andy was tempted to open one of the chocolates and gorge himself on it, but that's not what it was for. He quickly slid them into his school bag and left to do his chores.

Next morning Andy arrived earlier than usual in school. He sat on a bench in the playground and put one of the chocolates next to him. Carefully, he opened it and broke it into pieces.

It didn't take long for the first children to cast him a curious look. Two girls ambled closer, though pretending not to be interested in him.

"Want some chocolate?" Andy offered. The girls looked at each other. "I thought your birthday was in winter," one of them said.

"It's not my birthday," Andy replied, "just chocolate day." The girls bent down and took a piece each.

Meanwhile other children had smelled the treat and walked over to the bench. They still hesitated, so Andy held the chocolate up. "Want a piece, anyone?" he asked as cool as possible.

"Sure it's not poisoned?" Nils countered. "With you one can never be sure."

Andy was furious about this insult, but when Nils took a piece of chocolate and the other children followed his example, he decided to swallow his anger. At least they were accepting something from him. That was better than being ignored.

The last piece was gone when the bell rang. Andy felt
a little better entering the class this morning, that is,
until Chris bumped into his desk. "Ouch!" he mumbled,
obviously embarrassed, and for a moment their faces
met. It was Andy who looked away first. That lifeless
eye sent a shiver down his spine. How could he ever
get used to it? Out of an impulse Andy decided that
the other big chocolate was for Chris. He'd write a
note with it and slip it into Chris' bag when he wasn't
looking.

In fact, it took Andy four attempts to write his note.
In the end, he still wasn't sure, but decided that it
had to do. "Hi Chris," it read. "I'm really sorry that
you lost your eye in the fight. I wish it hadn't
happened. Andy."

After lunch, he lingered in the cloakroom until he was
alone. He quickly transferred the chocolate and the
note from his bag to Chris' and went out.

If he had hoped that his generosity in the morning
had won him friends, he was wrong. The others

ignored him or sent him packing, just as they had done
before. But Andy didn't give up so easily. He still had
some of his pocket money left and, once his
classmates got used to him giving out sweets, they
would gladly want him around.

The next morning Andy brought a bag of jelly beans
to school. Instead of sitting on the bench, he walked
around with it.
"Won the lottery or something?" one of the girls
teased him, but she took a handful nonetheless. Sure
enough, his classmates suddenly felt attracted to him.
Some of them even managed a friendly smile or said
thank you.

Then the bell rang and they all filed into the class.
But what was that? For a moment Andy held his
breath. On his desk lay the big chocolate with a note
from Chris, saying: "You can keep that! It won't bring
my eye back!"

Andy swallowed. He felt rejected and humiliated.
Everybody must have seen the note and knew of
Andy's attempt to make up to Chris. He quickly

grabbed the chocolate and put it into his school bag. Then he scrunched up the note and threw it in the bin.

At lunch time Andy once again sat on the bench sharing his chocolate. "If Chris is too stupid to accept it, let others enjoy the taste!" he told himself. Children came and went, and one boy even lingered for a while, telling Andy about a new engine he was going to get for his model railway. Andy had no interest in model railways, but he was glad that the boy spoke to him.

Andy's supply of sweets soon came to the attention of Mr Paterson. One day he held him back at break time to question him about it.

"Where did you get the money from, Andy?" he wanted to know.

"I plundered my piggy-bank," Andy said truthfully.

"Well, when I think of all the chocolate and candy you've brought to school the last week, your piggy-bank must have been bursting."

Andy nodded, stepping nervously from one foot to the other.

"Do your parents know you're spending your savings on sweets?" Mr Paterson asked.

"They don't care. It's my money," Andy quickly replied.

"And you're sure you have paid for everything?" Mr Paterson obviously didn't trust him.
"Of course I have!" Andy shot back.

"Hm. I still think I should have a word with your mother."

Andy nearly panicked. Of course, his seven kroner seventy five hadn't been enough to pay for all those sweets! When Mrs Sorvik did her accounts at the end of the month, she would be shocked to find out how much was missing.

"Anyway," Mr Paterson's voice rang in his ears, "you can't buy friends by giving out sweets. What about trying to be helpful instead?"

"Nobody wants my help," Andy replied.

"Well, you haven't really tried yet," Mr Paterson insisted. "You're not stupid, lad, so I'm sure you can think of better ways to endear yourself to your classmates than stuffing them with sweets." With this, he let Andy go.

This was the end of Andy's shoplifting and sweets sharing. During the next few days he was still worried to see Mr Paterson talk to his mum, but the teacher must have had too much else to do before the end of term. Then the holidays began.

7) A Friend at last

It was a hot day and after doing his chores on the farm, Andy was ready for a swim. Before he got near the place where the river widened into a pool, he could hear the screams and laughter of the other children enjoying a cool dip. For a moment Andy wasn't sure if it was a good idea to join them. They might make fun of him or even worse. But there was no other place along the river where he could enjoy a good swim. Everywhere else it was either too rocky and fast flowing or too shallow. Also, just above the pool was a footbridge, which served the hardier children as a diving board. No, there was no better place than that and what right did anyone have to spoil it for him? So Andy went straight to the river pool, stripped off to his boxers and ran into the water.

Ah, the cool stream was so refreshing! It washed the sweat off his skin and the tiredness from his brain. At first nobody took notice of him as he splashed through the water. Some of the smaller children even grinned at him when they saw his exuberant smile.

After a while, Andy decided it was time for a dive. He waded ashore and headed for the bridge where a few boys from his class were assembled. Three of them had already climbed the banister ready to jump. But the other two were suddenly barring his way.

"Get lost!" Per hissed at him, as Andy approached.

"We don't want you here!" Mattie added. Andy felt the familiar signs of anger rise in him. "It's not your personal bridge!" he shouted.

"No," Per was quick to answer. "It belongs to the people of the village, and you're no longer one of us."

His superior grin fuelled Andy's rage. He was ready to punch him but he knew that, with Mattie on his side, Per would easily defeat him.

"As long as I live here I can use the river like everybody else!" he shouted instead.

Meanwhile, the three boys who had been jumping off the bridge came clambering out of the water.

"Look who's trying to spoil our day!" Per called over to them, but the three didn't seem interested.

"He's not spoiling my day," one of them replied, as he squeezed past Mattie and Per. The other two followed him silently and Andy quickly seized the opportunity to slip in behind them. Before Per or Mattie could grab him, he had already climbed the banister and pushed himself off, diving into the pool.

The water embraced him as if to share his victory. But as soon as Andy came back to the surface he knew that he needed more than one dive to defeat Per and Mattie. So he made his way to the other end of the bridge and again hopped onto the banister before they could stop him. However, while he was still getting ready for the dive, the banister suddenly shook so violently that he lost his balance. He nearly fell backwards onto the bridge but managed to fling himself sideways and crashed into the river like a stone.

Even before he was out of the water he could hear the laughter and sneering from the bridge.

"How elegant, loser!" Per's voice rang above the general noise. "Practising for the Olympic show diving, hey?"

Andy was more than raging by now. He felt like a volcano ready to explode. Without thinking he grabbed Mattie, tore him off the bridge and threw him down the river bank. Then he approached Per, whose face had suddenly lost its cocksure grin.

"Come on then!" he growled, getting ready for the fight. "Come and gauge my eye out, you rat!"

Andy's hands turned into fists and he could hear his heart banging against his chest. He was ready to tear Per into pieces. But then he saw the post of the banister, and the next moment he heard a face scraping along it and that unearthly scream of pain Chris had let out when he fell.

"What's wrong? Lost your guts?" Per taunted. For a split-second Andy met his eyes. Then he turned and ran as fast as his trembling legs were taking him.

Andy didn't care where he was going as long as he fled from Per and Mattie and the other children of the village. Not that he was afraid of what they would do to him. No, their threats and taunting didn't scare him anymore. What scared him was his own reaction. How quickly could his temper lead him into another vicious fight and cause damage he could never repair! That lifeless eye in Chris' face haunted him day and night. What if Mattie had crashed onto a rock and broken his neck? What if they were right and he was too dangerous to live amongst them?

He ran until exhaustion forced him to slow down. By then he had already reached the edge of the forest and in front of him lay the vast open fell. Andy welcomed the cool breeze drying the sweat on his body. He carried on up the rocks and through the heather until he stood on top of the first hill. The view was hazy, and yet, the vastness of the empty land in front of him calmed him somehow and gave him hope that there was more to his life than the problems facing him in the village. He curled up on a soft patch of moss, watching a bird of prey circling in the distance. Slowly, his heavy eyelids closed and Andy fell into a sleep of exhaustion.

The cold must have woken him for, when he sat up, his body shivered and his legs ached with cramp. It was evening, although at this time of year the sun hardly disappeared behind the horizon. However, before Andy could get his bearings, he noticed something big

and shiny no more than ten yards away. He blinked and
stared, and the shiny thing seemed to stare at him as
well.
"An elk!" it suddenly flashed through Andy's mind.
"The white elk!" For a moment he held his breath.
What an awesome creature! The elk seemed to watch
him carefully, as if considering whether he could be
trusted or not. In the end he decided that the
motionless being on the patch of moss above him
didn't pose any danger and he lowered his head with
the huge antlers and resumed his meal.

Andy watched him for a while. Oh, how he wished Uncle Eddy was there with him to share the encounter!

"I knew all along that he was right," Andy thought. "I knew he'd really seen him."

He sighed. If only Chris and the others were here! Then they'd have to admit that they had been wrong. But the more Andy was thinking about his classmates, the less he was longing for their presence. "They'd probably have frightened the elk away by now, or he wouldn't have come in the first place," he thought. No, the elk was here for him, and for him alone. He had come to Andy to be his special friend.

After a while, Andy was aware how cold he was. How nice it would be to bury his body in the soft white fur! But when he stood up, the elk lifted his head and took a step back.

"Don't be afraid! I'd never ever harm you!" Andy called to him. He took a few steps in the elk's direction when the mighty animal suddenly lost its trust. Andy stopped, as the elk slowly retreated. Twice he looked back as if part of him wanted to stay with the boy. "I'll be back," Andy promised. "I'm your friend and I'll make sure nobody harms you."

The image of the deep blue eyes and the majestic antlers stayed with Andy as he hurried home. He longed to touch his shiny white fur and to curl his arms round his huge neck. How wonderful that must feel!
The village was quiet when Andy approached it. He quickly collected his clothes from the river bank and hurried home.

Dinnertime had long passed but his mum was still in the kitchen. "Where have you been, Andy?" she greeted him with relief. "I feared something had happened to you! Come and have a hot drink and I'll warm up some dinner for you."

Andy was touched by her care. Still full of his encounter with the elk he decided to share it with her.

"I saw the white one up on the fell, the elk Uncle Eddy was talking about," he began hopeful, but his mum interrupted him.

"What were you doing up on the fell on your own?" she asked, taken aback. This, Andy didn't want to tell her. While he was still groping for an answer, his mum said: "You know how dangerous it can be out there. Promise you won't go there again; not on your own."
Andy looked at his feet. He had just promised the white elk that he'd come back to him. How could he now promise his mum not to go up the fell again?

"Andy?" she asked, waiting for an answer.

He nodded, "Okay," though he didn't mean it.

8) The Hero

Twice more Andy managed to sneak away to the hills before the weather changed. He took his dad's binoculars as well as a jumper and a sandwich along but, when he got to the place where he had seen the elk before, there was no sign of him.

"Of course, he wouldn't hang around and wait for me," Andy told himself. "He'll have wandered somewhere else, wherever the grass is tasty." He held the binoculars in front of his eyes and scanned the open land in all directions. In some bracken below him he saw a movement, perhaps a fox or a weasel, and on the opposite slope a couple of mountain hare played in the sun. But wherever he turned the binoculars, they didn't show him what he was looking for. Andy took the glasses down and sighed. He was disappointed, having come all the way for nothing.

"How silly to think that the elk would be waiting for me!" he chided himself. For a moment he even wondered if their encounter had been just a dream. He sat on a rock and took his sandwich out but, before he could take the first bite, something to the left caught his attention. He trained the binoculars on the spot, still wondering if it was only his imagination. Slowly, the thick foliage of a coppice parted and out stepped the biggest and most majestic animal of the fell.

"He's coming back," Andy whispered. "He must be looking for me." Without hesitation he jumped up and rounded the hill which separated him from his friend.

The elk didn't see him until Andy was almost upon him. He looked up, a bunch of grass still hanging out of his mouth. Andy stopped, afraid to scare the elk with his hasty movement. As before, they stared at each other for a while, before the elk decided to carry on grazing. Andy inched his way forward. Now and again the elk stopped eating and made as if to retreat but, as soon as Andy stood still, he felt reassured that he wasn't in danger and resumed his meal. Finally, when Andy was no more than ten yards away, the elk turned round. Andy froze at once. He held his sandwich up like an offering and whispered: "Please, don't leave! I'm your friend."

The elk must have understood him for he went no further. Instead, he looked at Andy as if to say: "It's alright, boy, I'm not leaving you. I just have to get used to your presence."

In the end, Andy ate his sandwich and put his jumper on as the evening became fresh. He knew that he couldn't linger any longer since his mum expected him home for dinner. With a heavy heart he said good bye to his friend and promised to be back as soon as possible.

The next time the elk let him come even closer, though he made sure there was still a safe gap between them. He didn't seem interested in the apple and carrot Andy had brought and preferred to nibble the spongy moss. His white fur shone in the sun like a blanket of snow while each point of his antlers poked into the blue sky. Andy was awed just watching him so close. Was that how Uncle Eddy had felt the day they met? Andy would have loved to talk to Uncle Eddy, the only person who understood his feelings for the white elk. But he was away with the fishing fleet all summer, trying to make enough money to get by for another year.

When Andy came home that night dark clouds were rolling in from the west. The air felt heavy and it took him a long time to fall asleep.
A couple of hours later he was woken by thunder and lightning. He walked over to the window to watch the flashes flicker across the sky. Suddenly there was a loud bang. Andy nearly jumped out of his skin. A moment later he was sure he could smell smoke. Had the lightning struck one of the outbuildings of the farm? He scanned the darkness outside, but didn't see smoke or flames. Should he call his mum?
He crossed his room and opened the door, nearly bumping into her. Helga was also up.

"I can smell fire," Andy said. "I think one of our outbuildings has been struck!"

They all ran down the stairs and out into the yard, but everything seemed fine. Suddenly Helga pointed in the direction of their neighbours. "Look!" she shouted.

They all stared at the orange flames shooting into the night sky.
"Quick! We'll have to help them," mum said, and despite the fact that they were all wearing night clothes, she ushered them across the field to the neighbours' farm.

When they got there, Mr Rimland, his wife and his two sons were already busy with the water hose. They assured Andy's mum that the fire was under control and, after a short time, the flames were extinguished.

"I'm glad it wasn't worse," Andy's mum spoke to Mrs Rimland. "If it had struck the barn with all the fresh hay..." They talked for a bit while Mr Rimland and his sons were examining the damage.

"We were lucky," Andy heard him say. Thunder and lightning were moving away, but in their wake followed a heavy squall of rain.

"We'd better get home!" Andy's mum called, and the three of them ran across the field to take shelter in their own house.

Later, when he had changed into dry pyjamas and was comfortably tucked in his bed, Andy's mind was still preoccupied with the fire. Part of him was disappointed that the Rimlands hadn't needed their help. In his mind he imagined their house having caught fire with the family trapped inside. He, Andy, was the first one on the scene. Without hesitation, he burst through the flames and fought his way upstairs. One of the boys lay unconscious on the landing with his brother bending over him. Andy quickly rushed into their room and tore the sheets off their beds. The flames were advancing behind him, while he knotted them together and tied them to the windowsill. Although the boys were both taller than him, Andy managed to carry them one by one down the sheet-rope. Once he had safely deposited them on the grass, he rushed back into the burning house to rescue their parents. Mrs Rimland scratched and kicked him in her panic, but Andy ignored the pain. He also ignored his singed skin and his burning throat. If it wasn't for him, the Rimlands were going to die, but Andy was ready to give his own life for them.

As soon as all four inhabitants were safely out, the roof started to cave in. Andy had been just in time. Only then did other people arrive on the scene. A fire engine noisily rushed around the corner and an ambulance stopped in the drive. The paramedics quickly examined the five people on the grass and decided it was Andy who had suffered worst. They took him to hospital and cared for his wounds. One by one and in small groups, people from the village came to visit him. They were all full of praise for his heroic rescue of the Rimlands.

"If it hadn't been for you, there would only be ashes left of them," Mr Paterson said. "I'm proud of you, Anders. I can see that you took to heart what I said about helping people. Well done!"

Andy basked in their praise and admiration. Finally, he was accepted back into their midst. Even Chris came to his hospital bed, but seeing his face Andy couldn't help but look away. Suddenly his heroic dream came to an abrupt end. He hadn't rescued the Rimlands. He didn't even need to help put out the fire. He wasn't a hero at all. Andy sighed. If only he could show the people in the village that he was one of them! If only he had the chance to prove it!

With a heavy heart he turned to face the wall and tried to go back to sleep.

9) Caught

The next day Andy was heading for the shop. His mum had sent him for some groceries since she and Helga were busy making jam. Andy hadn't been to the shop for a while as he was still finishing off the sweets he had intended for his classmates.

He soon had his shopping basket filled with the sugar, pasta, flour and washing-up liquid written on his mum's shopping list when he found himself unexpectedly in front of the chocolate shelf. He noticed some new varieties and felt his mouth water. He knew he should have gone straight to the check-out before the temptation became too much, but he didn't. Instead, he counted the money in his mum's purse, wondering if she would notice if he spent a little extra on a treat for himself. He didn't think she had counted every kroner, but at the same time he couldn't bring himself to steal from his mum. It was much easier to slip the chocolate under his shirt as he had done so often. Putting his groceries on the counter, he heard the door open and turned round to see who was coming in. With a jolt, he recognised Mr Paterson.

"Enjoying your holidays?" the teacher called over. Andy nodded and turned back to the check-out. At this moment his shirt came loose and something slid half-way out. Andy quickly pushed the chocolate back, but it was too late. Mrs Sorvik had already seen it. Her eyes narrowed and she stopped scanning the flour.

"Take that out!" she demanded angrily.

Andy nervously looked at his feet. "What do you mean?" he tried to stall.

"You know exactly what I mean!" Mrs Sorvik shouted at him. With trembling fingers Andy pulled the chocolate out of his shirt and put it on the counter.

"And why was this not in your basket?" Mrs Sorvik wanted to know. Andy didn't know what to answer, so he kept quiet.

"Don't tell me that's the first time you're stealing from my shop!" Mrs Sorvik ranted at him.

"I remember you coming in here almost every day for a while, and now that I think of it, it makes sense that my accounts didn't add up at the end of the month. A lot of those missing sweets never went through the till!"

Andy was ready to defend himself, but when he looked up, he saw Mr Paterson staring at him. There was no point denying what he had done. The teacher came closer and asked Mrs Sorvik: "How much money does he owe you?"

"What?" Mrs Sorvik was taken aback. "I'll have to look it up, but I can tell you, it's a fair sum."

Mr Paterson spoke again. "I suggest you find out and Anders will either pay with his pocket money or work it off in your shop."

"I'm not having that boy ever enter my shop again!" Mrs Sorvik exploded. "I'll go to the police and let them deal with it! It's high time they do something about that... that criminal!"

Andy wished he could simply vanish, evaporate like a puddle in the sun. A criminal. Was that what people thought of him?

Meanwhile Mr Paterson did his best to calm the shopkeeper down. "Let me talk to his parents," he said. "I should've done it as soon as I saw him give out those sweets at school." He sighed. "He was trying to appease his classmates with them, but I told him this wasn't the right way to make friends."

In the end, Mrs Sorvik gave in. She let Andy pay for his mum's groceries and found in her accounts the sum for the missing sweets. Andy couldn't believe it came to over forty kroner. He was sure someone else had stolen some of it, but he knew better than to protest. The words *criminal* and *police* were still ringing in his ears, so he was glad that Mr Paterson had taken the situation into his own hands.

He took Andy home, where his mum and sister were busy in the kitchen.

"I'm sorry to disturb you, Mrs Larsen, but I need to have a word with you about your son," he said. Andy's mum looked up from the pot of jam she was stirring.

"Helga, take over for a minute," she called to her daughter, dried her hands on her apron and led Mr Paterson out of the kitchen. Andy wasn't sure what to do. He felt like running off into the woods, but the rain had just become heavy again.

"Put the sugar over there. We'll need it in a minute," Helga said to him as if nothing was the matter. Andy put the shopping bag on a stool and opened it. While he took the sugar out, Helga asked him to pass her one of the jars. He handed it to her and went back to unpacking the groceries.

"Wet the cloth for me, please," she said a minute later, and so brother and sister were working together like a team when their mum came back. She didn't talk to Andy straight away, but sent him to fetch more jars from the storeroom. After that, she found other tasks for him to do, until it was time for a lunch break.

Andy had no appetite. The longer his mum let him wait, the worse he felt. What was she going to say and do? He didn't have enough money to pay Mrs Sorvik back immediately. Besides, paying her back was only half the problem. She had banned him from her shop, the only shop in the village, and she might still consider involving the police. How would his dad take this, his own son being a criminal?

Finally, while Helga was carrying the dishes away, his mum took Andy aside. First she just looked at him, as if unsure how to begin. Then she cleared her throat and took a deep breath.

"Your teacher has told me the whole story, with you stealing sweets and giving them to your classmates." She shook her head in disbelief. "How could you do something like that, Andy! Did you really think that would bring you friends?" Again she shook her head and sighed. "Oh Andy, you've just gone from bad to worse. What shall we do with you?" Her voice suddenly began to tremble and she buried her face in her hands.

Andy felt worse than ever. Had she shouted at him or given him a punishment, he could take it. He could feel sorry for himself and be angry with the whole world. But to see his mother so distraught only added to his guilt. For the first time he understood that his actions did not only affect his own life, but that of his family as well. Did Helga have to put up with taunting because her brother was a criminal? How did his mum feel when the whole village was talking about *that boy who made Chris lose his eye?* What had his dad had to endure when his workmates found the story in the newspaper? Did people blame his parents for what had become of him?

"I'm sorry, mum," Andy heard himself whisper. "I'll pay it all off. I'll do lots of chores for you, if you want, and dad can sell my fishing rod and the new flies." He sighed at the thought of losing them, but he was ready to do anything to put things straight. "I promise, I'll pay it all off, and I'll never ever steal again in my whole life." Suddenly, his mum looked up, and through her tears Andy could see the hint of a smile.

"Oh Andy, I'm so glad you're feeling sorry, and I'm sure we'll find a way to sort this out." She wiped her face on her apron and straightened up. "Right now you can go and pick the rest of the black currants, and later I'll make a list with chores that'll keep you busy for a while." They both got up from the table. "We have to wait for dad to come home before we can pay back Mrs Sorvik, but in the meantime I want you to write her a letter of apology – your best handwriting and spelling, you hear me?" Andy nodded, and a moment later he found himself in his mum's embrace. It had been ages since she had last hugged him and Andy had to admit that it felt warm and safe.

10) Sinking

Andy had never seen his dad so angry before. He confronted him in the yard when Andy came back from the hen house, holding a basket with eggs in his hand.

"There you are!" he roared at him like a hungry lion. He grabbed Andy by his shoulders and shook him so hard that he dropped the basket.

"What do you think you're doing, stealing from the shop? You useless piece of dirt! Here I am, toiling away all week to earn a decent living for my family, and you have nothing better to do than gauge people's eyes out and go shoplifting!"

His words hit Andy worse than fists. He had wanted to apologise, to work hard to make things good, but his dad didn't give him a chance. He had already ticked him off as a *useless piece of dirt*. In the end, he gave Andy a shove that landed him on the ground and spat: "Get out of my sight!"

Andy didn't need to be told twice. As soon as he was back on his feet he ran towards the forest. Tears were flowing down his cheeks, tears of rage and hurt. He didn't know what was stronger, his anger towards his dad or the contempt he felt for himself. In any case, he had to get away, as far away as possible from the place where he had messed up his life.

When his lungs were burning from the effort of running, Andy slowed his pace, but he didn't stop until he reached the top of the hill where he had met the white elk. Never had he been so desperate for a friend, for someone to whom he still mattered. He scanned the land in front of him, but the hazy sky didn't let him see far. The elk could be anywhere out there. He could have wandered miles across the mountains and might even have returned to the National Park by now. After all, Andy hadn't visited him for almost a week. The elk might have thought he had lost interest in him.

"But he could still be nearby," Andy told himself in order to keep up his spirits, and he set out into the mist to look for him.

The ground was still wet from the recent rain. Here and there the long cotton grass indicated a particularly swampy area, forcing Andy to find a way around it. He not only looked out for the elk himself, but for any signs, like hoof prints or flattened grass that told him he had been around. At one point he came across a small bush with juicy orange berries which he recognised as edible. He picked the ripe ones, suddenly aware how hungry he was. Would he ever have dinner with his family again, he wondered.

Something moved in front of him. Andy froze. He thought it was a grass snake, but before he had time to identify it, it had already vanished. While he was still staring at the ground in front of him, he made out some large hoof prints.

"Could be the elk," he reasoned. "Or maybe a reindeer."

He bent down to have a closer look. Then he got up to see where the prints were leading. For a while he followed what he thought was a track, winding itself around a hillock and descending into a wide bowl. Andy wasn't only hungry, he was tired as well and, when the mist became thicker, he started to feel cold.

"It's useless," he told himself. "I'll never find him. He's probably walked off, looking for a better friend than me." Downhearted, he trudged on, no longer trying to follow a track or heading in any particular direction. It didn't matter where he was going. His life didn't matter anymore. He had no friends, and his own family no longer wanted him around. He might as well get lost in the vastness of the fell.

While he was still stumbling onwards like this, his left leg suddenly gave way under him. Andy quickly shifted his weight onto his right side, but he lost his balance and fell headlong into a swamp. Getting up was not easy, as the slimy mass was tugging at his body. When he finally managed to stand he realised that both his legs were stuck. He used all his strength to free them, but the bog was stronger than him. Close to panic he reached as far as he could, but the long grass at the edge of the bog was too far away from him. Without a chance to pull himself out he remained a prisoner of the bog.

"Calm down," Andy told himself. "Don't panic, or you'll be doomed." A minute ago he had been convinced that his life was useless, but being stuck in this place with no prospect of escape suddenly brought back his desire to live.

"I have to get out of here! There must be a way out!" he thought desperately. However, his efforts to pull out his legs only made him sink deeper. In the end he could no longer stop the panic.

"I want out here!" he shouted at the top of his voice.
"Help! Help me! Mum! Dad! I need help!" His arms
slashed wildly at the gooey soup around him. "I want
out here! Mum! Dad! Please, help me!!!" Suddenly he
broke down. Heavy sobs shook his body, while tears
streamed down his face. Of course, his mum and dad

couldn't hear him. There was nobody near enough to hear his cries. He was alone, entirely alone. Nobody even knew where to look for him. Once his body had been swallowed by the swamp, they would never know what had happened to him. The thought made him cry even harder. Perhaps the people in the village would be glad to be rid of him. His own family might be better off without him. This might be his punishment for what he had done to Chris.

No, such ideas were too horrible to dwell on. Andy had to cling to the slightest hope he could muster. But what hope was there?

Meanwhile, the bog reached up to his waist. Andy shivered with cold and fear. Once more he looked around him for anything he could hold on to and pull himself out, but there was nothing within his reach. He felt utterly forsaken. Where had he heard that word before? "Forsaken... God-forsaken..." Had God forsaken him? He wasn't even sure if he believed in God. Andy had never really thought about it. Yes, he knew that some people prayed to God and went to church and read the Bible. But he had never been much interested in all this – until now. Suddenly, the idea of an invisible, almighty God watching over his creation seemed the only hope Andy had. But would this God want to help him? Was he not as angry with Andy as everybody else? After all, fighting, lying and stealing were not exactly the kind of things God approved of. Andy sighed. He knew he couldn't earn God's favour, just as he couldn't give Chris a new eye. What he needed was forgiveness. It was as plain as that.

"God!" he called into the sky. "I'm sorry for all the mess I've made! I'm really sorry! Please, please, forgive me and help me out of this bog! Please, God, there's nobody else. I need you to help me!" Tears were streaming down his face again, as his body slid deeper into the bog. Andy's arms hung limp to his sides. He knew he could do nothing to free himself.

Andy was still crying when the sound of crunching feet mingled with his sobs. He looked up and through a curtain of tears he suddenly saw something huge and white emerge from the mist. For a moment he held his breath. "The elk. The white elk," he whispered.

First he wondered if it was just a mirage, wishful thinking or some trick of his imagination. But the elk came closer. His split hooves and long thin legs were made to wade through swamp. He went right up to Andy and let him fling his arms around his broad neck. Then he pulled, carefully, to make sure Andy didn't lose his grip. Bit by bit he pulled him out of the bog until both of them were back on firm ground. Andy was so exhausted that he could neither sit nor stand. He just lay in the grass with the elk standing nearby, watching over him.

"You really heard me," Andy whispered when he found his voice again. "You really heard me and you rescued me." He wasn't even sure whether he was addressing God or the elk or both of them. In the end, he decided that God had heard his prayer and had sent the elk to save him from drowning. He had given him a new life. Andy was filled with awe. As if to celebrate the miracle with him, the clouds lifted and the sun came out, drying Andy's sodden clothes and warming his body.

He must have slept for a while, for the sun had moved far towards the horizon. The elk was grazing peacefully a short distance away and lifted his head when Andy sat up.

"I wish I could eat grass like you," Andy called to him.

His stomach was rumbling and he felt thirsty, too, but there was nothing for him out in the fell. If he wanted to eat, he had to go back to the village.

The thought of facing his dad made him tremble. He had called him a useless piece of dirt. How could Andy ever share a home with him again? He was wondering whether to bypass his village and walk on to the next one. Sure, he had no money to buy food, but he could just nick some...

No, that would only get him into trouble again. It would be his old life all over. That's not what God had rescued him for. There must be a better way, and

since God had done one miracle for him, he might as
well ask for another one. It took Andy a while to
overcome his hurt and his pride, but in the end he
meant what he prayed. "Please, God, help dad and me
to make up again." With this, he stood up, said good
bye to his friend, the white elk, and began the long
walk back.

11) A Fresh Start

The church clock struck three times when Andy came near the village. During the light summer nights it was hard to tell the time, but Andy hadn't thought it was that long after midnight. He was wondering how to get into the house, if everybody was asleep and the front door locked.

"I'll try to wake Helga," he decided in the end, but when he approached the farm, he saw that the light was on in the kitchen. Someone was moving behind the net curtains. Andy recognised his dad and suddenly his feet stopped.

"What if he's still furious?" he thought. "What if he doesn't even let me in?" It wasn't as if Andy could just go to a friend's house. He didn't have any friends. This was the only place where he could find food and shelter.

Still unsure how to approach the house, he noticed his mum's face at the kitchen window. She must have seen him, for she disappeared again and a moment later she opened the front door, calling his name. Andy didn't hesitate any longer. He ran to the door and flung himself into her arms.

"Andy, we were so worried about you!" she told him. "We were looking for you all over the place. Your dad even went up to the fell, but in the mist he couldn't see far."

When Andy looked up, he found his dad standing right beside his mother. "Come in, son," he said, and those words were the best Andy had heard in a long time.

While his mum hastily warmed up a meal for him, his dad sat at the opposite end of the table, playing nervously with his fingers.

"Well," he finally said, "I'm glad you've come back." His voice sounded thin and rusty, and he cleared his throat before he continued: "I didn't really mean what I said." He struggled for words. "I mean, I was angry. Of course, I was angry with you, and I'm sure you know how that feels." For a split-second he looked Andy in the eyes. Then he carried on: "Your mum's right. The best way forward is to let you work to pay off your debt to the shop. And regarding Chris and his injury, we have to give him time. There's nothing you or I can do about his eye, so there's no point punishing you for it."

His mum put a steaming plate in front of Andy and he hungrily began to eat. His parents watched him for a while, talking about chores on the farm and the weather and dad's upcoming holidays. When Andy had finished he suddenly felt so tired that he could hardly keep his eyes open. His dad wished him a good night while his mum took him upstairs where she helped him undress.

"Goodness me! Your socks and trousers look as if you dragged them through the mud," she commented, yet more curious than angry. "I should stick you straight in the bath, but I'm afraid in your state you'd drown."

Andy could hardly make sense of her words. As soon as he was tucked under his blankets he was fast asleep.

When Andy woke up, it was already past lunchtime, but nobody scolded him for it. His mum cut some of his favourite cheese for him and Helga offered him some chocolate pudding she had made.

Later his dad invited him for a walk round the fields to make sure the fences weren't broken and the animals were all well. Andy enjoyed the walk. His dad pointed some wild flowers out to him, explaining what medical powers they had, and he showed him how to tell the direction without a compass by looking at the growth of lichen on the trees. This was his old dad, the way Andy remembered him before he had taken the job in town. If only the farm alone could support them! Then his dad didn't have to toil away in the tractor factory all week with only a small bed-sit to come back to at night. Perhaps when Helga and Andy were old enough to earn their own living, dad could come back to the farm. In fact, Andy might be able to buy him a couple more fields to grow crops in. He imagined how proud his dad would be of him. But in order to earn enough money he'd need to get a good job. And in order to get a good job he needed qualifications, which meant a big improvement in his school work. Until now, Andy had never seen much point in his education. He couldn't imagine anything but farm or factory work, or perhaps he simply hadn't had any ambitions. But since he was given a second chance at life, it had become more special to him and he was inclined not to waste it, but to live more thoughtfully.

The following week passed without any incidents, and yet, somehow every moment felt special to Andy. Again and again his mind replayed his sinking in the bog and the miraculous rescue. Again and again he marvelled at the sudden change that had taken place between his dad and him. And again and again Andy was overwhelmed by awe, when he thought of God's power and personal care. He prayed more often, not just asking for help and thanking God for his miracles, but simply sharing what he saw and felt, thought and experienced. It was so good to have a friend he could talk to at any time and wherever he was, a friend who knew his past, present and future, who forgave him and opened new ways for him which Andy had never thought possible. He would even have liked to go to church on Sunday, had it not been for Chris' dad standing in the pulpit. Andy knew that Chris had not forgiven him and that his family still bore him a grudge. Perhaps his dad was right and it took time for them to change their mind.

Having been busy on the farm all week, his mum let him have a day off on Saturday. His dad was fixing the barn door and Helga was getting ready to meet her friends, so Andy decided it was high time to visit **his** friend again out on the fell. He made up a packed lunch and asked his dad for the binoculars.

"Going bird-watching, are you?" he teased him, knowing very well that Andy had never been patient enough to wait silently in some bush or hide-out.

"No, I just like to look out for enemies," he replied, pretending he was playing some game in the woods. Andy had considered telling his dad about the white elk. Perhaps he would go up with him and Andy could introduce him to his special friend. But something had stopped him. Was it the fear that someone would harm the elk if word got round that he lived up on the fell? Or was their friendship so precious to Andy that he didn't want to let anyone else into it? In any case, the white elk was still his secret and, since his parents would not allow him to hike up onto he fell, he rather kept quiet about where he was off to.

The binoculars proved essential, since the elk had wandered far off onto another hill. Andy only spotted him because his white fur sparkled in the sun. He picked his way carefully round the worst of the swamp, wherever possible sticking to rocks and heather. When he came within about ten yards of the elk, he slowed down.

"Hello, my friend," he called quietly. The elk looked him up and down, as if to make sure this was the same boy he had rescued from the bog.

"It's me," Andy assured him, taking a step forward. The elk seemed slightly uneasy. After all, Andy had read that elks were shy and solitary creatures and, although these days their only enemies were men with rifles, they were always on alert.

When the gap between them had narrowed to about five yards, the elk took a step back. Andy stopped. Then he had an idea. He opened his rucksack and took one of his sandwiches out.

"Would you like a bite of this?" he asked the elk, while holding the sandwich out to him on the palm of his hand. The elk stretched out its head and sniffed, but he wasn't interested enough to make a move forward. Andy took a bite of his sandwich to show the elk that it was food.

"It's delicious!" he assured his friend. "It has butter and cheese on it and a piece of lettuce." Then he had another idea. He rummaged in his rucksack for the apple and, when he found it, he held it out to the elk.

"Do you prefer this?" he asked him. The elk moved its nostrils to catch the smell.

"It's nice and juicy," Andy told him and to make sure
the elk understood, he took a bite out of it and
crunched it noisily between his teeth. With the rest
of his apple on his palm he slowly approached the elk
until he nearly touched his nose. The elk sniffed
noisily. Finally he opened his mouth and reached for
the apple. Very carefully he picked it up. Andy felt a
warm shiver run down his spine, when his soft lips
touched his palm. The elk had accepted his gift. He
had decided to trust him. Slowly he munched the

apple, all the while looking at the boy, who had given it to him. This was a very special moment for both of them. Although the elk had let him come close before, when he pulled him out of the swamp, it was this gesture of trust which sealed their friendship for good. Andy took another step forward so he could stroke the elk's neck. He felt his gentle breath on his face as the elk took in his scent. The warm feeling in his back stayed with Andy while they stood there together, surrounded by barren hills and wet grassland. Fragments of clouds sailed past on the blue sky and the occasional hum of an insect or the call of a bird penetrated the air. This was as close as Andy had ever come to happiness. And suddenly it was as if someone was smiling down on them from above, sharing their joy.

"My God," Andy whispered, "thank you so much!"

And in his own way the great white elk joined in his praise.

12) New Friends

For the next two weeks his dad was home on holidays. It was the busiest time on the farm, and they all worked hard together.

One morning his dad asked Andy to hold a ladder for him while he climbed up onto the roof of the house to wedge a couple of slates back in their place. Andy held on to the ladder until his arms hurt. Then he decided to simply lean against it with his back. He was wondering what took his dad so long up there when he saw something fall out of the beech tree in front of him. Andy looked closer and recognised a fledgling bird. The tiny thing was flapping its fluffy wings but couldn't get off the ground. It called anxiously for its parents. Instead, the farm cat came stalking around the corner of the barn, obviously attracted by the helpless cries. Andy watched as the cat came closer. When it had almost reached the tree, he shouted at it and tried to shoo it away, but the cat took no notice of him. Andy searched the ground for something he could throw at the cat. There were a few stones not far from him. He quickly dashed for them and tossed them at the cat. Scared, the cat stopped in its tracks before running back towards the barn. The fledgling bird was safe for now, but suddenly the ladder behind him began to move. Andy threw himself at it, trying to steady it, but his dad at the upper end had already lost his balance.

"Hey! What's happening!" he shouted down, desperately clinging to the swaying rungs. With all his strength, Andy could just prevent the ladder tipping over sideways but he couldn't straighten it again.

"What's going on, son?" his dad called down to him. "Are you still there?"

Andy didn't know what to answer. He just wanted his dad to come down safely. Finally he saw his feet appear over the edge of the roof. The ladder began to sway again. His dad stopped and turned his head to see what was going on below him. "Hold on!" he called to Andy and carefully made his descent. When his feet were nearly level with Andy's head, the ladder suddenly lurched sideways and clattered to the ground. Andy was thrown off balance while his dad jumped to safety.

"You alright, lad?" he asked when Andy slowly got to his feet. He nodded, too shaken for words.

"What happened?" his dad wanted to know. What made the ladder suddenly come loose?" Andy looked at the ground. He didn't want to admit that he had let go of the ladder to help the bird. His dad could have fallen and broken his neck, only because he hadn't followed instructions. So he shrugged his shoulders and wiped his dirty hands on his trousers. But his dad didn't let it rest with that.

"Come on, it was perfectly stable while I fixed those slates, and all of a sudden it began to slide sideways."

He looked down at Andy who couldn't meet his gaze. "Did you let go of it?" he suddenly asked straight out.

Andy wanted to deny it, but the lie got stuck in his throat.

"Did you?" his dad demanded, his anger rising. Andy knew he had to say something. He pointed to the fledgling bird that was still chirping under the beech tree. "The cat tried to get it and I had to throw stones to make it go away," he explained with a feeble voice.

"You let go of the ladder to save that little bugger?" dad asked incredulously. "A half-dead bird is more important to you than your own father?"

"It only took a moment," Andy tried to defend himself. "I didn't think the ladder would..."

"Then it's time you start thinking!" his dad spat at him. "Luckily I managed to get down before it collapsed!" With that, he bent down to pick up the ladder. Andy offered to help, but his dad shooed him away. "Go and get Helga," he growled. "At least I can depend on her to do what she's told."

For the rest of the day Andy tried to avoid his dad. He felt shaken and hurt and wished he could do something to show that he wasn't useless. However, by evening his dad must have got over his shock, for he invited Andy to go fishing with him, something they hadn't done together in a long time. While they were standing in the river, casting their rods, a huge heron came gliding over their heads. They followed it with their eyes until it disappeared behind the trees.

"Quite amazing," his dad called over.

"Awesome," Andy replied.

For a long time they caught nothing. It was almost time to go home when Andy felt a strong tug on his rod. He gave out some line before reeling it in again, but whatever he had caught nearly pulled him off his feet. "Dad!" he shouted, afraid to lose the battle and his rod as well. His dad flung his own rod onto the riverbank and waded over to help him.

"That's a real bugger!" he agreed, when he got a grip on Andy's rod. It took both of them to reel the fish in and, as soon as he appeared on the surface, Andy stepped forward to grab it with his hands. He slipped and fell into the water, but he didn't let go of the fish. Together they managed to drag it ashore where Andy's dad picked up a rock to end its struggle.

"Boy, what a catch!" he said in admiration, and his praise meant more to Andy than the fish itself.

Soon they had a small fire going, drying Andy's clothes and roasting the flesh of the trout. The smoke kept the beasties away who would otherwise have bitten them insane.

While they were still waiting for the fish to cook, a small boy appeared at the riverbank, followed by an older boy and a man. Andy recognised them as the Bornholms, who lived further down the valley, just outside the village. Alfie was two or three years younger than him, and his brother, Sigi, was a class ahead of Andy.

"I see you were lucky tonight," their dad said, when he saw the fish roasting over the fire.

"Andy caught him," his dad answered. "We were just about to give up when he hooked this bugger." Andy felt the eyes of the two boys on him as they admired him for his catch.

"What kind of flies are you using?" Sigi wanted to know and Andy showed him. They discussed the advantages and disadvantages of certain types of bait and Andy realised how long he had missed such ordinary conversation with his peers.

In the end, they invited the Bornholms to share the fish with them, which tasted better than anything Andy had eaten in a long time.

A few days later, Sigi and Alfie called at his house to ask if Andy wanted to come swimming with them. They had each got a set of snorkels and flippers – a present from an aunt who had been visiting – and promised to let Andy have a try. He could hardly believe their kindness. It was just another of the many miracles God had recently worked in his life.

When they approached the river pool there was already a crowd of children enjoying the water. They hung their clothes and towels on a branch and surged forward into the coolness of the river. How wonderful it was to wash off the sweat and dust and to feel new energy pumping through one's body! Andy found himself squealing with joy, something he hadn't dared to do for the past weeks.

Suddenly, a couple of boys from his class approached him. "Hey, get out!" they shouted, and one of them grabbed his arm. "This is for decent people, not for psychos like you!" Together, the two boys dragged him out of the water, but they hadn't counted on Sigi. As soon as he saw what was happening to Andy, he followed him ashore and confronted the boys.

"Why did you do that?" he asked calmly, looking them straight in the eyes. Sigi was tall and well-built and the boys were obviously afraid of him.

"He should keep away from here after what he did to Chris," one of them said rather nervously. Sigi's next question surprised them all. "Have you ever had a fight?" he asked the boys. They wondered whether he wanted to pick one with them. Of cause, they had fought many a time. Dragging Andy out of the water was almost like starting a fight.

"So you have," Sigi answered for them. "You're just lucky that nobody got seriously hurt in it." They knew he was saying this to refer to Chris. Then his voice took on a harsher tone. "Come on, how much longer are you going to pick on Andy for something he has long regretted happening?" The boys didn't say a word. They nervously trod on the spot, obviously embarrassed and longing to get away.

"Lay off, will you?" Sigi demanded. "If you want to help Chris, then invite him for a swim and help him to find his confidence again." With that, he took Andy by his shoulder and walked him back into the water.

It was the last time the boys picked on him, and from then on Andy had no more qualms about going for a swim and dive at the river pool.

One day his mum insisted to take him to the shop.

Meanwhile, Andy had paid off his debts for the stolen sweets and had sent Mrs Sorvik several gifts of fresh fruit and home-made jam to make amends. It was time she forgave him. First Mrs Sorvik looked rather sceptical when Andy and his mum entered the shop. She did her best to keep an eye on him, while Andy helped his mother to tick off the items on her list.

"Did you enjoy the raspberries Andy picked for you?" Mrs Larsen asked, when they came to the check-out. Now the shopkeeper could no longer avoid letting go of her grudge.

"Well, yes, they were very nice," she admitted and finally said the words Andy needed to hear. "Thank you. That was very thoughtful of you. I see you have changed for the better."

Andy nodded, feeling embarrassed as well as relieved. Mrs Sorvik rung up their groceries and Andy's mum handed her the money while Andy reached for the shopping bags. They said good-bye and went on their way.

"I think that's sorted now," his mum said when they were walking home. Andy hadn't realised how much stress and worry the situation had caused her, and he was as glad as she was that things were finally sorted. He vowed never to steal again, however tempting it might become.

13) The Hunt

It was during the final week of the summer holidays that a rumour went through the village of some hikers who had spotted a white elk on the Borgefell. When Andy heard of it he first felt a sense of pride. Now they all had to admit that Uncle Eddy was not drunk when he reported his encounter with the white elk. But his pride was short-lived. What would happen to his special friend now that others were aware of his existence?

The next rumour worried him even more. People were talking about going up to see him with their own eyes. "I don't think they just want to stand there and admire his white fur," Andy's dad said one night at the dinner table. "That fur is worth a fortune! All they have to do is take it off him, before the park officials can get him back to safety."

Andy nearly choked when he heard this. "You mean, killing him?" he asked, once he got his breath back.

"How else would they get his fur off!" Helga put in.

"I'm sure the likes of Mr Legland and Mr Svenson are already polishing their rifles, ready to be first on the scene." Andy was shocked. He hadn't realised that his elk was in such imminent danger. What if the men had already gone to shoot him?

Suddenly he jumped up. "Please, may I be excused?" he asked his parents.

"What, no pudding for you tonight?" his mum said surprised. Andy shook his head. "Well, go then," she added, and he didn't hesitate.

A few minutes later, Andy raced towards the woods. All he had taken time to pack were his dad's binoculars, a jacket and a couple of apples. They were rattling in his rucksack as he hurried along the familiar path.

Soon he was out of breath and slowed his pace. For a while he searched the ground in front of him for recent footprints, but the earth was too dry to give anything away.

When Andy crossed the stream where the forest gave way to the open fell, he bent down for a drink. He could have done with a short rest, but the thought of his friend being threatened by gunmen drove him on.

Once he reached the top of the hill Andy took out the binoculars and scanned the land in front of him. First he didn't see any movement but, when he looked closer, he detected something to his right. A head emerged from behind a rocky outcrop but it wasn't what he was looking for. For a moment Andy held his breath. Then another head emerged and shortly after he recognised the bodies of two men. They were carrying something over their shoulders which looked like hunting rifles.

"No!" Andy hissed. "Go away! You're not going to kill my friend!" He wanted to run down to the two men and stop them from carrying out their cruel plans. But at that moment he spotted another movement out on the fell. He trained the binoculars on the place. It was the white elk, majestically stalking through the long cotton grass without the slightest idea of the danger he was in. In that instant Andy knew what he had to do. He had to reach his friend before the men had seen him. Then they would flee together towards the National Park and safety.

Andy turned left and half-ran, half-skidded down the grassy hillside. In his hurry he nearly forgot to watch out for bog holes, but when the water splashed around his ankle, he looked more carefully where he put his feet. All the while he kept praying, urging God to protect his friend and to help them escape from the hunters.

When the ground in front of him rose again Andy momentarily lost sight of the elk. A stabbing pain in his side forced him to slow down. He used his hands to pull himself up on rocks and heather but, once he reached the top of the rise, his heart nearly stopped. The hunters were walking straight in the direction of his friend, while the elk, to Andy's frustration, was unknowingly walking towards them. His only chance of survival depended on Andy's speed. If he didn't get to him before the men, the white elk would meet his death.

Without hesitation, Andy started running again. He skirted round bog holes and jumped over small streams, his heart pounding, his side aching and his lungs pumping as fast as they could.

The two men from the village couldn't believe their luck. Hiding behind a rocky outcrop, they watched as the king of the fell slowly strode towards them, his fur glittering in the sun like a silver necklace and his antlers poking into the sky like a crown. He stopped for a moment, stretching his long nose in the direction of the men, but their scent was hidden from his nostrils.

"Wait until he's a bit closer," one of the hunters whispered to his friend. They both had their rifles ready, watching their target through the viewfinder.

Suddenly the elk turned his head in the other direction and began to walk away from them.

A shot rang through the air, immediately followed by another one. A flock of birds flew out of a nearby thicket, shrieking in alarm. Startled, the elk took off across the fell. Twice he stopped to look back, confused and bewildered, wondering what had happened to his friend, but his instinct told him to put as much distance as possible between himself and the humans who had suddenly made that dreadful noise.

Meanwhile the hunters had thrown their rifles in the grass and were bending over the unconscious boy. "He ran straight into my bullet!" Bjorn Svenson repeated over and over. "I didn't see him coming! I was firing at the elk, when the boy ran in front of him!"

Arne Legland's rifle had also gone off, though the bullet went way off to the side. Like Bjorn, he was shocked about what had happened, but his mind was clear enough to tell him what to do next.

"He's alive, that's for sure," he said. "We'll have to carry him to the village and get a doctor." He turned

Andy over and saw a red patch expanding from his right shoulder. Lifting Andy's shirt, it was obvious where the bullet had struck him. Arne took a handkerchief out of his pocket to pluck the wound. "I'll carry him first," he offered. "You take my rifle."

Bjorn did as told. He was still going on about the boy having run into his bullet and where he could suddenly have come from, until Arne told him to save his breath.

Several times they stopped to swap their load, with Andy remaining unconscious. When they came to the edge of the forest the sun dipped behind the horizon but, at this time of year, the daylight never faded completely. However, engulfed by the trees, it was darker and they had to take care not to stumble over roots or dead branches.

"What are we going to say?" Bjorn asked, aware that the episode could land him in prison.

"Let's just say we were hunting rabbits and foxes out there," Arne replied. "There's nothing wrong with that and, as you say, the boy ran straight into your path. It's not as if you aimed the shot at him."

When they finally reached the village, they went to the first house to phone for an ambulance. While they were waiting for it to arrive, Andy briefly gained consciousness, but the pain in his shoulder and chest was too much, and soon his mind shut down again.

14) Forgiveness

The next time Andy woke up he found himself in a strange room. Looking down his body he noticed several tubes connected to his wrists. He tried to move his arms. The left one seemed fine, but the right one didn't want to obey him. Next he tried to wriggle his toes and move his legs. They seemed alright. His head hurt slightly and he felt very thirsty.

By now he was aware that he lay in a hospital bed and slowly he began to remember. He knew he had been running through the long grass towards his friend, the white elk. Had he been in time? Andy hoped that the elk was safe and well. He turned his head to see if there was a glass of water on his bedside table. At that moment the door opened and a nurse came in.

"I'm glad you've woken up," she said, smiling at Andy and adjusting one of the tubes going into his wrist. "How are you feeling?"

Andy blushed. The nurse looked pretty young, not much older than his sister Helga, and he wasn't used to talk about his feelings, especially with a girl. "Well," he reminded himself, "she needs to know how my body's doing." So he told her that he had a slight headache, couldn't move his right arm and was thirsty. She left to get him a drink, her long braid dancing on her back.

When she had handed him the cup of water, she explained about the wound in his right shoulder. "Part of the bone and muscle got damaged, but it would've been much worse if the bullet had struck you a few millimetres to the left. If it had injured your spine, you'd find yourself paralyzed."

Andy swallowed. The bullet? What was she talking about? Once more he wriggled his toes and moved his legs and his left arm to make sure they were functioning. Slowly the memory of the hunters on the fell came back to him. He remembered running as fast as he could to protect his friend, but he couldn't remember what happened next. He had been lucky, though. He could have been paralyzed or even dead.

But what about the elk? Was he injured or had Andy been in time? He wanted to ask the nurse but he wasn't sure that she knew about the elk. What had the two hunters told the medics about Andy's injury? At least they had not abandoned him but made sure he got help. After a while he fell asleep again.

The next time Andy woke he heard hushed voices around him. When he opened his eyes he saw his parents standing at the side of his bed.

"Oh, Andy! Have you woken up at last?" his mum asked, as if it wasn't obvious. He noticed deep rings under her eyes and knew she must have been crying hard. His dad, too, looked rather grave, nervously plucking at the hat he was holding in his hands.

"You gave us such a fright," he said to Andy. "What came into you, running straight into the path of the hunters?" He shook his head. "They could have killed you, do you hear me? It was a very stupid thing to do."

Andy didn't know what to reply. He was desperate to know if the elk got away, but he was afraid the question would make his dad only angrier. He didn't understand why Andy had risked his life to protect the elk. He didn't know about their friendship and that the elk had saved his life. Andy sighed and closed his eyes. He would have to wait until Uncle Eddy was back, or perhaps Helga could fill him in when she came to visit.

The news about the shooting accident was all over the village and beyond. When Helga read in the paper that the two men had been after rabbits and foxes, she felt anger rise in her chest. "What a cheek!" she whispered. "Since when would you shoot a rabbit or fox a metre above the ground?" She shook her head. "Don't tell me Andy was crouching in front of you! He wouldn't risk his life for a daft rabbit! It was the elk – the white elk – you were after!" She suddenly jumped up and threw the paper onto the table. She knew she had to do something, for her brother's sake. She had to make sure the truth came out and, although she was very nervous about making the phone call, there was nothing to stop her.

The police woman listened patiently, taking notes of what Helga was saying and promising to follow it up.

The next visitor at Andy's bedside was a tall lady in a blue uniform. First he got a fright when he saw the police logo on her shoulder. Would they arrest him for trying to save his friend? But the lady looked friendly, not angry, when she asked him to tell her what he remembered. So Andy began with the rumours that the white elk had been sighted on the fell above the village and that some people were keen to get his skin. "I wanted to protect him. That's why I ran up there," he explained.

"How did you know the rumours were true?" the police woman interrupted. Andy blushed. Would she believe his secret friendship with the elk? He stammered: "I'd seen him myself, and so had my uncle." His fingers nervously played with the buttons on his hospital gown.

"So you wanted to protect him from being shot," the police woman stated.

"Yes, I thought I could chase him away, back to the Park where he'd come from," Andy carried on. "I saw him, and then I saw the men with their rifles. So I ran even faster and suddenly... suddenly it all went black."

The police woman wrote down his statement and handed it to Andy to read and sign it. Before she left, he asked tentatively: "Do you know what happened to the white elk? Has he been seen again?" She shook her head, but promised to look into it and let him know when they had any news.

A week later Andy was allowed to go home. He still had to rest a lot, and his right shoulder was in a caster. The new school year was about to start. Andy felt a knot in his stomach at the thought of having to face up to his classmates again. Although they had stopped being openly hostile to him since the day Sigi confronted them, nobody had offered to be his friend either. Andy was afraid to be ignored again and left out, and the memory of his loneliness and boredom was almost more painful than his damaged shoulder. He prayed about it, sharing his fears with God, but they carried on troubling him. Then, one day, something extraordinary happened.

"Andy, there's a visitor for you!" Helga called from the front door, while he was resting in bed. He was wondering who this could be. "Maybe Sigi? Or Mr Paterson?" The door of his room was slightly ajar, when Helga pushed it open to let the boy in. Andy looked up and dropped the book he had been reading. For a moment his heart seemed to stand still. What did he want? Why had he come? Andy turned his head to avoid the staring eye and looked at the wall.

"I've come to say sorry," Chris said quietly, taking a small step forward. "I want to say sorry for having been so nasty to you since our fight," he mumbled, not looking at Andy either. For a long moment, there was an awkward silence between them. Then Andy slightly turned his head and said: "You know, I'm very sorry about your eye. I never meant it to happen."

"I know that," Chris replied. "But I meant to hurt you afterwards. I was so angry, I wanted to punish you for the pain you'd caused me." He sighed and tentatively took another step forward. "But actually, I punished myself by doing so, because it made me so bitter, just living for revenge." Again, silence fell over the room. Then Andy suddenly looked up. "What made you change your mind? I mean, what made you decide to forgive me?" The whole scene seemed so strange, that for a moment Andy wondered if he was dreaming. How he had longed for Chris to accept him again! He had even been willing to give his own eye, if that could restore Chris' sight. Had his dad been right that Chris just needed time to come to terms with what had happened?

"Well, the other day in church," Chris began awkwardly, "when I was bored with my dad's preaching, I looked at the pictures on the wall. There's one of Jesus on the cross, saying: <Father, forgive them, for they don't know what they're doing.> That's what he prayed for those who crucified him." He lifted his head and looked out of the window, but Andy knew that his mind was not on the trees and the sun rays filtering through the leaves.

"When you think how much pain he must have suffered and knowing he had to hang there until he was dead..." He shook his head. "If Jesus could forgive those who had done that to him, then he'd surely help us forgive one another." He paused for a moment, before he added: "Because he shares our pain, we don't need to inflict pain on those who caused it."

Andy nodded. He thought of how much God had already helped him. Would he have done that if he was still holding a grudge against him? No, God had forgiven him. Jesus had made up for all his wrongs. He was glad that Chris had discovered this, too. Now they could both live in peace and everything would come right. Chris looked round, and for the first time Andy was able to meet his gaze without feeling sick.

"I'm really sorry you lost your eye," he said. "What's it like? Does it hurt a lot?"

"Not anymore," Chris replied. "And I'm getting used to it. I no longer bump into things all the time. The doctor says that my brain is adjusting to my new sight and that soon I'll be scoring goals again and diving off the bridge and things like that." He no longer looked awkward, and his voice sounded like the old confident Chris. "What about your shoulder?" he wanted to know. "Is it going to heal completely?"

"I hope so," Andy replied. "It still hurts a lot, but I'm so lucky the bullet didn't hit my spine."

Chris nodded. "Bjorn Svenson might go to prison for this," he said. "In any case, he's already lost his rifle licence, and so has Arne Legland. Of course, the pair wasn't after rabbits! Everybody knows that they wanted the white elk." He suddenly stopped, as if he was looking inward again.

"You know?" he finally carried on. "Your Uncle Eddy was right. If only I'd believed him, we'd never have had that fight..."

"I'm not sure," Andy put in. "Perhaps we'd have fought about something else. I always used my fists when I was angry. But things have changed..."

Chris stayed on for a while, and when he left, the boys no longer felt awkward with each other. They had made peace. Andy stopped dreading the beginning of the new school term. A huge burden had been lifted from his back; another miracle in answer to his prayers.

15) Safe and Free

Andy's arm was still in a sling when Uncle Eddy returned from the sea. One Friday afternoon his old Landrover noisily turned into the farm yard, leaving a cloud of dust behind. Andy came running out of the hen house where he had been collecting eggs.

"Uncle Eddy!" he called, when the vehicle stopped. He flung himself at the driver's door and tried to open it with his left hand. A moment later Uncle Eddy climbed down the steps of his Landrover and embraced his nephew in a bear hug. Andy winced. His wounded shoulder was still tender to touch.

"How's it going, old boy?" Uncle Eddy asked with his deep voice.

"My arm's getting better, and school's quite cool this year," Andy answered. Uncle Eddy went to get some bits and pieces out of the boot before they made their way to the front door.

That night's dinner was even more of a feast than the usual Friday welcome for dad. Uncle Eddy kept them all captivated with his tales from the high seas. No wonder they took ages to finish their meal!

Afterwards, Andy went back for the basket of eggs before helping his sister with the dishes. Finally he was free to look for his uncle again.

The two men were sitting in the living room, nursing a beer, when Andy came in. They were talking about the farm and work in general. Andy listened for a while, until he began to feel bored and was wondering whether to leave. Just then, however, Uncle Eddy changed the subject.

"I've heard about the two poachers who were trying to shoot our elk," he said, shaking his head. "I told the park authorities in spring that I'd seen him up on our fell, but they wouldn't believe me. Everybody thought I'd made it up."

"I believed you," Andy quickly piped up. In fact, if he hadn't stood up for his uncle, a lot of things would never have happened.

"Unfortunately, you did," his dad added quietly.

"And later, I saw him for myself." For the first time, Andy related the whole story of his friendship with the elk, including the last-minute rescue from the bog hole. His dad looked at him, as if he didn't quite believe what Andy was saying, but Uncle Eddy had no doubt that he was telling the truth.

"Their hoofs are split, so they can walk through swamp without getting stuck," he explained, "and I've heard that the white one has a very distinct personality. Elks are solitary creatures, but that one was partly reared by one of the park rangers and is therefore not as scared of humans as the others. He must have sensed that you came as a friend and not to harm him."

Andy nodded. Uncle Eddy had always understood him better than his dad. After a moment of silence he asked: "Do you know where the white elk is now? Was he... was he injured?"

Uncle Eddy's face told him the good news before he put it into words. "The only one injured was you, Andy. You took the shot that was meant for the elk, and that's quite something, I'd say."

"It's the most stupid thing to do!" Andy's dad put in angrily.

"It's a noble thing to give your life for a friend," Uncle Eddy corrected him. Before they were able to break out into a hot argument, Andy asked again: "Do you know where he is now?"

Uncle Eddy nodded. "When the police told them about the poachers, the park rangers finally came over to look for their precious elk. In fact, they found him close to the place where you were injured that night, as if he was looking for something... or someone."

Andy swallowed the tears that suddenly threatened to well up in his eyes. The elk had been looking for him. He had not forgotten their friendship. Would he still recognize him after several weeks?

"Did they bring him back to the National Park?" Andy wanted to know.
"Yes, they did," Uncle Eddy replied, "and I tell you what..." He paused for a moment, as if considering how best to announce his plans. "What about setting off early tomorrow morning to drive to the Park? We can stay overnight in one of the huts and, if we're lucky, we'll find your friend to say hello to him."

Andy could hardly believe what he heard. To meet his friend, the white elk again? "Wow!" was all that came over his lips. "Wow!"

His dad needed some convincing, but in the end he agreed to let Andy go. "Make sure you bring him back, though," he warned Uncle Eddy, "my son, of course, not the elk!"

It was late morning, when the Landrover turned off the road and onto a bumpy track which ended at the National Park Office. Uncle Eddy parked at the side of the low building. It was a clear day with a hint of autumn in the air. Andy climbed out of the Landrover and pulled his hat over his ears to keep out the cold wind. Then he followed Uncle Eddy into the building.

Once they had got permission to hike in the Park and to spend the coming night in one of the small shelters on the fell, they retrieved their rucksacks from the back of the Landrover and set off. Because Andy's right shoulder was still tender, he adjusted both straps to sit on his left one. It was a bit awkward at first but he soon got used to it.

Uncle Eddy was a brisk walker, but Andy found that he no longer struggled to keep up with him. His hikes up the fell during the summer must have strengthened his muscles and his lungs. Uncle Eddy had showed him on the map where they were going. It was an area of the Park where the elks were known to gather at this time of year to find a mate.

"I'm not sure about our white friend," Uncle Eddy admitted, "but he might well be there, too."

It was a perfect day for spotting wildlife. Each hill granted them a wider view over the surrounding fell, and through their binoculars they watched mountain hares play in the sun, a fox sneak out of a thicket and disappear behind a rock and a bird of prey circle above them in the blue sky. They came across a lizard sunning itself on a warm stone and Andy nearly stepped on a grass snake, which slithered in front of him through the heather. Later, Uncle Eddy pointed out hoof-prints of elk and deer and marks, which might have been made by a bear.

"Did you ever meet a bear?" Andy wanted to know.

Uncle Eddy nodded. "Once, and I'm glad to say that the bear must have been well fed or else I would've been its breakfast."

They had just eaten their lunch, sitting on a rocky outcrop, when Andy noticed some movement below them. He trained his binoculars on the spot and saw several female elks.

"Well, I guess the males can't be far away," Uncle Eddy said, and soon they were on their way again.

Before long, the ground in front of them was teaming with hoof-prints, excrements and bits of fur left by elks. When they rounded another hill they saw several males, two of them attacking each other with their huge antlers. Andy was wondering if his friend was fighting like them, but he couldn't imagine it. "He's always been so peaceful..." he thought.

In the evening they came to the tiny shelter which had just enough room for them to sleep in. Uncle Eddy took out his little gas cooker and sent Andy to fetch water from a nearby stream. After dinner they watched the sun set behind the hills, painting the sky with a tinge of pink, before the light faded and darkness fell around them. Snug in their sleeping bags they saw the first star appear on the night sky. Then the roaring of the stags began to fill the air. The distant noise kept them awake for a while but in the end their tiredness overtook them.

The morning was chilly and the ground was wet with dew. Andy splashed some cold water into his face to wake up properly. The stags were finally quiet, but instead the birds gave their morning concert. From somewhere a cuckoo was shouting its two notes into the air. Uncle Eddy prepared breakfast and, as soon as they had eaten and packed their rucksacks, they were on their way again.

As the day went on they came across several groups of elks and some on their own, but all of them had brown fur, as was usual for elks. Andy had almost given up meeting his friend again. He was deep in his thoughts when Uncle Eddy suddenly touched his arm. Without a word, he pointed to the left. Andy turned his head, and even without using his binoculars he could clearly make out the shiny white body. For a moment, he just stood and watched. Then he slowly lowered his rucksack into the grass and placed the binoculars on top of it. He wanted to meet his friend the way they had always met, unencumbered and free.

The elk noticed him as soon as Andy started to walk towards him. He lifted his head, but his legs didn't move. Andy walked slowly, even though he felt the urge to run. He spoke quietly to his friend to let him know that he came in peace.

When they were about twenty metres apart, the elk suddenly took a step back. Andy stopped. "What is it?" he asked. "Are you afraid of me?" They looked at each other. "I'm your friend, remember?" Andy took a step forward, then another one. This time, the elk let him approach until they were almost touching. Andy stretched out his hand to let the elk take in his scent. "See, it's me," he whispered, before he let his fingers glide through the white fur. One more step and they were side by side. While Andy stroked his fur, the elk gently nibbled his hair. They were still friends.

Suddenly Andy was aware of a rustling noise in a nearby thicket. A moment later the head of a big brown elk cow appeared from behind the branches. Andy froze. His friend stopped nuzzling him and took a step back.

"I see," Andy whispered when he found his voice again. "You've found a girl friend." He felt a mixture of awe and disappointment. The white elk looked at him, and, as before, in his dark eyes Andy found something of himself.

"I'm glad you're back in the Park where you're safe and free," he said with a heavy heart. "And I'm glad you've found a mate." He nodded, more to himself than to the elk.

"I've also found some mates again," he told his friend. "But you'll always be special to me and I'll never forget you." His voice began to quiver but he carried on: "You were there for me when nobody else wanted to be my friend. You saved my life and let me save yours. You'll always have a special place in my heart."

Tears blurred his sight, as his fingers touched the white fur one last time. "Thank you, my friend." The elk let out a deep sigh before he turned and slowly walked towards his mate. Andy wiped the tears from his eyes and made his way back to his uncle. For a while they didn't speak a word. When Andy was finally ready to talk, he said: "I'm glad we met, even though it hurts to part again."

Uncle Eddy put his hand on his shoulder. "That's the way of life," he sighed.

"Yes," Andy agreed, "there's only one friend who'll never ever leave us."

"And who's that?" Uncle Eddy wanted to know.

"Jesus," Andy said, and when he looked up, the rays of the sun painted a smile on his face and his eyes shone with a deep peace.